The Boxcar Children Mysteries

The Boxcar Children
Surprise Island
The Yellow House Mystery
Mystery Ranch
Mike's Mystery
Blue Bay Mystery
The Woodshed Mystery
The Lighthouse Mystery
Mountain Top Mystery
Schoolhouse Mystery
Caboose Mystery
Houseboat Mystery
Snowbound Mystery
Tree House Mystery
Bicycle Mystery
Mystery in the Sand
Mystery Behind the Wall
Bus Station Mystery
Benny Uncovers a Mystery
The Haunted Cabin Mystery
The Deserted Library Mystery
The Animal Shelter Mystery
The Old Motel Mystery
The Mystery of the Hidden Painting
The Amusement Park Mystery
The Mystery of the Mixed-Up Zoo
The Camp-Out Mystery
The Mystery Girl
The Mystery Cruise
The Disappearing Friend Mystery
The Mystery of the Singing Ghost
Mystery in the Snow
The Pizza Mystery
The Mystery Horse
The Mystery at the Dog Show
The Castle Mystery
The Mystery of the Lost Village
The Mystery on the Ice
The Mystery of the Purple Pool
The Ghost Ship Mystery
The Mystery in Washington, DC
The Canoe Trip Mystery
The Mystery of the Hidden Beach
The Mystery of the Missing Cat
The Mystery at Snowflake Inn
The Mystery on Stage
The Dinosaur Mystery
The Mystery of the Stolen Music
The Mystery at the Ball Park
The Chocolate Sundae Mystery
The Mystery of the Hot Air Balloon
The Mystery Bookstore
The Pilgrim Village Mystery
The Mystery of the Stolen Boxcar
The Mystery in the Cave
The Mystery on the Train
The Mystery at the Fair

The Mystery of the Lost Mine
The Guide Dog Mystery
The Hurricane Mystery
The Pet Shop Mystery
The Mystery of the Secret Message
The Firehouse Mystery
The Mystery in San Francisco
The Niagara Falls Mystery
The Mystery at the Alamo
The Outer Space Mystery
The Soccer Mystery
The Mystery in the Old Attic
The Growling Bear Mystery
The Mystery of the Lake Monster
The Mystery at Peacock Hall
The Windy City Mystery
The Black Pearl Mystery
The Cereal Box Mystery
The Panther Mystery
The Mystery of the Queen's Jewels
The Stolen Sword Mystery
The Basketball Mystery
The Movie Star Mystery
The Mystery of the Pirate's Map
The Ghost Town Mystery
The Mystery of the Black Raven
The Mystery in the Mall
The Mystery in New York
The Gymnastics Mystery
The Poison Frog Mystery
The Mystery of the Empty Safe
The Home Run Mystery
The Great Bicycle Race Mystery
The Mystery of the Wild Ponies
The Mystery in the Computer Game
The Mystery at the Crooked House
The Hockey Mystery
The Mystery of the Midnight Dog
The Mystery of the Screech Owl
The Summer Camp Mystery
The Copycat Mystery
The Haunted Clock Tower Mystery
The Mystery of the Tiger's Eye
The Disappearing Staircase Mystery
The Mystery on Blizzard Mountain
The Mystery of the Spider's Clue
The Candy Factory Mystery
The Mystery of the Mummy's Curse
The Mystery of the Star Ruby
The Stuffed Bear Mystery
The Mystery of Alligator Swamp
The Mystery at Skeleton Point
The Tattletale Mystery
The Comic Book Mystery
The Great Shark Mystery

THE GREAT SHARK MYSTERY

created by

GERTRUDE CHANDLER WARNER

Illustrated by Hodges Soileau

ALBERT WHITMAN & Company
Morton Grove, Illinois

Activities by Rebecca Gomez
Activity illustrations by Alfred Giuliani

ISBN 0-8075-5532-0

Published by Scholastic Inc., 557 Broadway, New York, NY 10012, by arrangement with Albert Whitman & Company. BOXCAR CHILDREN is a registered trademark of Albert Whitman & Company.

1 3 5 7 9 10 8 6 4 2

Printed in the U.S.A.

Contents

CHAPTER 1

Danger in the Deep

"Help! It's going to get me! It's going to eat me!" screamed Benny Alden. He looked back at the giant shark swimming toward him. He swam away from it as fast as he could, pulling his hands through the water and kicking his legs harder and harder. But each time he glanced back, the shark was closer. It was gaining on him.

Six-year-old Benny gasped for breath. How much longer could he swim before the shark caught him?

Suddenly, Benny felt something grab him. He closed his eyes tightly. His body began to shake.

Had the shark gotten him at last?

From far away, Benny heard a voice calling, "Benny! Benny!"

Benny opened his eyes.

"Benny, wake up!" cried the voice. "You're dreaming!"

Benny slowly began to realize where he was. He was in bed, and his twelve-year-old sister, Jessie, was standing beside him, shaking him gently by the shoulders. The clock on his bedside table said it was midnight.

"What's going on?" Benny asked, rubbing his eyes.

"You were having a nightmare," Jessie said. "Was it a shark again?"

Benny nodded, shivering. "It almost got me this time!"

Jessie sat down on the edge of the bed and put her hand gently on Benny's arm. "It was only a dream," she reminded him. "You're safe in bed."

Benny noticed his grandfather standing

beside the bed, wearing a blue bathrobe over his pajamas. Benny and Jessie lived with him, along with their fourteen-year-old brother, Henry, and ten-year-old sister, Violet. After their parents had died, Benny, Violet, Jessie, and Henry lived for a while in an old abandoned boxcar in the woods. Then their grandfather found them and they went to live with him in his big white house in Greenfield. Mr. Alden even brought the boxcar to the backyard for the kids to play in.

"I should never have let you see that movie, *Danger in the Deep*," Grandfather said. "I had no idea it would be so scary."

Violet poked her head into the room. "The shark dream again?" she asked, yawning.

Jessie nodded.

"Poor Benny," said Violet. "That's the third time this week."

"I'm never going to the beach again!" Benny said.

Grandfather frowned, thinking about something.

"Will you be able to go back to sleep now?" Jessie asked Benny.

Her little brother nodded.

Grandfather bent to give Benny a kiss and tucked the covers snugly around him.

"Can we still finish our checkers game tomorrow morning?" Benny asked.

"First thing," Mr. Alden said as he turned out the bedside lamp, but he sounded distracted. Benny wondered what Grandfather was thinking about. But he only wondered for a moment, because he quickly fell back to sleep. This time there were no more dreams of sharks.

The next morning, when Benny woke up, he could smell pancakes cooking. He quickly dressed and made his bed, then ran downstairs to the kitchen. "Good morning, Mrs. McGregor!" he called out as he poured himself a glass of orange juice.

"Good morning, Benny," replied the housekeeper, with a friendly smile. She handed Benny a plate piled high with steaming hot pancakes.

"Thanks," he said, sitting down to eat. "Where's Grandfather?" Benny licked a drip of syrup off his fork. Mr. Alden was usually the first one up.

"He went out," Mrs. McGregor said.

"So early?" Benny said.

Mrs. McGregor looked at the clock. "It's not so early, young man. You slept in today."

"Where did he go?" Benny wanted to know.

"He didn't say," said Mrs. McGregor. "He was having his coffee and reading the paper as he does every morning, when suddenly he jumped up and made a phone call. Then he went out."

The corners of Benny's mouth turned down in disappointment. "He promised we'd finish our checkers game first thing this morning."

"Don't worry, I'm sure he'll be back soon," said Mrs. McGregor.

Henry came into the kitchen. "Good morning," he said, serving himself some pancakes. He sat down at the end of the table, moving the morning newspaper out of the way.

"Hey, what's this?" he asked, pointing to the paper. It was opened to a page with a large photograph at the top. "Something about a shark."

"What?" Benny said, coming over to take a closer look. The photograph showed a giant shark with a huge mouth and rows of sharp, pointed teeth.

Henry read the headline aloud: " 'Great White Shark Caught.' " He read the article quickly. "It says that an adventure park in Florida just brought in a great white shark."

"Sharks again?" asked Jessie, coming into the kitchen with Violet.

Henry handed Jessie the newspaper. She looked at the article. "It says that it's very unusual for a great white shark to be in an aquarium."

Just then the door opened and Grandfather came in, whistling, an envelope tucked under his arm. "Good morning," he said. He waggled his eyebrows and smiled at the children.

"What have you been up to?" Violet said.

"I just made a little visit to the travel agent," Mr. Alden replied. "We're going on a trip."

"We are?" Henry said.

"Where to?" asked Jessie.

"Here are the tickets — take a look!" Grandfather flipped the envelope onto the table.

Benny snatched up the envelope and pulled out the tickets. "F—fuh . . . flo . . ." Benny sounded out.

Jessie helped him, reading the ticket over his shoulder. "Florida?" she asked.

Grandfather nodded. "Ocean Adventure Park."

"We were just reading about that place in the paper," said Henry.

"I know someone who works there," Grandfather explained. "Her name is Emily Ballard and she's the daughter of a good friend. This morning I called and asked if you kids could spend a little time there — help out, learn about the animals. You see, I'd been wondering how to help Benny get over his fear of sharks. When I saw that article I had the answer. We leave this afternoon."

"This afternoon?" said Jessie.

"Emily said to come as soon as possible, so you'll get a chance to see the great white shark," Grandfather explained. "She said they may not be able to keep it very long."

"But do we have to go so soon?" Benny asked nervously.

"The sooner the better," shouted Henry. "We're going to Florida!"

Jessie, Violet, and Henry raced out of the kitchen excitedly. Only Benny remained with Grandfather. He did not look happy.

Grandfather pulled out a chair and sat down beside his grandson.

"What's Ocean Adventure Park like?" Benny asked in a quiet voice.

Mr. Alden put his arm around his grandson. "It's a wonderful place," he assured him. "They have all kinds of underwater creatures — fish, penguins, manatees, dolphins. You'll meet people who love working with all of them — even the sharks. You'll learn all about the animals, and that you don't need to be afraid of the water." He paused. "Sometimes, if you're scared of something, learning about it can be a great way to overcome your fear."

Benny looked up at his grandfather. He didn't seem convinced. "All right," he said. "I guess I'll go pack."

"You don't have to pack right this minute," Grandfather said. "We've got a checkers match to finish."

Benny broke into a smile. "That's right!" he said. But as he got up to get the board, he couldn't help seeing the newspaper lying on the table. He took one look at the gaping jaws in the photograph and shivered.

That evening, the Aldens stepped off the plane in Florida. A cheerful young woman approached them. She had long blond hair and bright blue eyes, and her skin was deeply tanned.

"I'm Emily Ballard. Are you the Aldens?" she asked with a friendly smile.

"Yes, we are," said Grandfather. "I'm James Alden. I've heard so much about you from your dad. It's nice to finally meet you."

"I've heard a lot about you, too," Emily said. Then she turned to the children. "You must be Henry, Jessie, and Violet."

"And I'm Benny," Benny piped up.

"Come on, let's go get your luggage," Emily suggested. As they headed down the walkway, she and Grandfather talked about her father and how he was doing.

At a pause in the conversation, Violet asked, "Emily, what do you do at the park?"

"I'm the head animal trainer. I help care for the animals, feed them, and teach them tricks for the shows," Emily said.

"Wow, that sounds cool!" said Jessie.

"It is," Emily said. "I love what I do. It's the best job in the world."

When they arrived at Ocean Adventure Park, the Aldens found it was not at all what they'd expected. They couldn't help noticing how run-down and shabby everything was. The buildings needed fresh paint and the fences needed to be repaired. Weeds grew up over the edges of the cracked side-walk.

"Looks like this place could use a little work," Mr. Alden said.

"You're right about that," Emily said. "Unfortunately, there just isn't enough money in the budget right now for that."

"Really?" Grandfather asked. "Is the park having trouble?"

"We've had a hard time competing with all the fancy theme parks nearby," Emily said.

"I bet you won't have a problem getting people to come now that you've got a great white shark," Henry said.

Emily frowned. "Yes, it's nearly empty now, since the park has just closed for the day. But it was quite crowded earlier."

Henry noticed Emily's frown. "I would think you'd be happy about that."

"It's not that I don't want the park to do well," said Emily. "It's just . . . that shark is a living, breathing animal. But to some people here, all that matters is how much money it's going to make."

Grandfather was silently studying Emily's serious face.

"What do you mean?" Violet asked.

"Oh, I shouldn't have said that. . . ." Emily shook her head as if to clear away whatever she'd been thinking about. "Come on, we'll drop off your bags and then I'll give you a tour."

They were passing the main office building when someone called out, "Hello!"

The Aldens looked behind them to see a young man wearing a bright blue baseball cap coming up the path. He seemed to be calling out to them, but the Aldens didn't recognize him.

"Is that someone you know?" Violet asked Emily. "He seems to be trying to get your attention."

Emily glanced back at the man and frowned. "No one I know," she said, turning to a gate with a sign that read EMPLOYEES ONLY. She pulled a white card key out of her pocket and slipped it in a slot beside the gate.

As Emily led them down the path on the

other side of the gate, Violet stopped and looked back. The man was standing at the gate, which had closed and locked behind them. He was still watching them. Who was he, and why was he trying to get their attention?

CHAPTER 2

The Great White Shark

Violet hurried to catch up with the group. They had stopped in front of a small cabin. Emily was saying, "Here's where you kids will be staying."

"What about you, Grandfather?" asked Benny.

"I'll be staying with Emily's father," Mr. Alden told them. "I'll head over there after we see the shark."

"My dad's house is about an hour from here," Emily said. "But if you kids need anything, my cabin is right next door. Your grandfather said you like to be on your own."

"We do," said Jessie.

"You live right here in the park?" Henry asked.

"Yes, it's much easier, since I work long hours," Emily explained. "I have no commute to work, and I don't have to worry about paying rent."

The Aldens entered their cabin and found themselves in a small sitting room with a couch, chairs, and a table. At one end was a kitchenette with a small refrigerator and stove. Off the sitting room were two bedrooms, each with a pair of beds.

"Violet and I will take this room," said Jessie, claiming the room on the left. "You boys can take the other room."

"Okay," said Henry, putting his suitcase down.

"Now can we see the shark?" Jessie wanted to know.

"Sure," said Emily. She led the way out the door and back up the path. Violet was curious to see if the man was still at the gate, but he was gone.

The Aldens strolled along next to Emily. They passed several different exhibits. Some were open tanks, like the tropical fish pool. Others were buildings marked with signs such as PENGUIN HOUSE or MANATEE HAVEN.

"I love penguins!" Violet said.

"I've never heard of a manatee," said Benny.

Emily laughed. "I can see this is going to be a busy week," she said. "Don't worry, we'll spend time with all kinds of different animals."

At last they came to a building with a large sign that simply read SHARKS! in menacing black letters. "The smaller sharks are in there," Emily explained. "But we needed a larger tank for the great white, so it's in the old Beluga whale tank over there."

The Aldens followed Emily toward a large enclosure. A hastily painted sign on the outside read COME FACE-TO-FACE WITH A GREAT WHITE SHARK!

"Are you ready?" Emily asked.

The Aldens looked at one another. Grandfather smiled, and the older three children nodded eagerly. Benny took a deep breath and then slowly nodded.

One by one, the Aldens stepped through the doorway, with Benny bringing up the rear.

Ahead of them was a huge glass tank. The Aldens stepped to the glass and peered in. In the dim light, it was at first hard to make out what was in the tank. But then a shape began to move toward them, slowly, slowly. It seemed to be swimming straight at them.

The Aldens were face-to-face with a real live shark. And there was nothing between them and the shark but a pane of glass.

As the shark glided by, it opened its mouth slightly. The Aldens caught a glimpse of rows and rows of sharp, pointed teeth.

"Look at all those teeth," said Violet.

"And look how big they are!" said Jessie.

"Sharks have several rows of teeth," said

a voice behind them. "Thousands of teeth altogether. When some fall out, others fill in. And their teeth can be as big as three inches tall."

Emily and the Aldens turned around to face the speaker. He was tall, dark-haired, and muscular. His skin was weathered from many years in the sun and wind. He smiled kindly at the Aldens, then turned to Emily. "Are these the visitors you told me about?"

"Yes, Mac," she replied, motioning to each one as she said their names. "This is James Alden, and his grandchildren Henry, Violet, Benny, and Jessie. This is Mac Brody, animal curator here at the park."

"Wait a minute," Henry said, looking at Mr. Brody and then at Emily. "Did you say *Mac Brody*? I think I read a book about you. *Tales of* . . ."

"*The Sharkman*?" Mr. Brody chuckled. "That's my autobiography. I'm glad to hear somebody's reading it."

"Wow! Did you really do all those things, Mr. Brody?" Henry asked.

"I did indeed," he replied. "And you can call me Mac."

"You swam with sharks?" Henry said. "And survived an attack by a great white?"

Mac nodded. "Yes, a great white shark once tried to kill me, and now I'm trying my best to keep another great white alive."

Benny looked up at Mac, his eyes wide.

"What do you mean?" asked Violet.

"This shark got caught in a net and was brought here. But great whites don't do well in aquariums," Mac explained. "They're very mysterious animals — extremely sensitive to electrical currents and other changes in their environments. So they have to be taken back to the ocean or . . ." Mac's voice trailed off.

"Or what?" asked Violet.

"Or they die," said Mac.

"Now you're trying to convince children?" said a voice. Walking quickly toward them was a tall woman with curly black hair. She was wearing a business suit and high heels.

"Anita," Mac said. "This is James Alden,

along with his grandchildren, the kids who are staying in the visitors' cabin. This is the director of the park, Anita Carver," Mac continued.

The Aldens all smiled. "It's nice to meet you," Mr. Alden said.

"Thanks for letting us come visit," said Henry.

"I hope you enjoy your stay," said Ms. Carver. She smiled, but her tone was curt. She didn't seem to want to chat. "Now, if you'll excuse us a moment." She and Mac stepped off to one side. Emily and the Aldens stood by the tank, watching the shark swim. But they couldn't help overhearing the conversation nearby.

"I got your note," Ms. Carver was saying. "We can't just let the shark *go*."

"If we don't, it will die." Mac's voice was angry. "A great white won't survive in captivity."

"Can't we just build a bigger tank or something?" Ms. Carver asked.

"No great white has ever survived in an aquarium for more than a few days," Mac replied. "Anyway, it would cost a lot of money to build a bigger tank. And we don't even have enough money to fix up the tanks we already have. We simply can't afford to keep it."

"We can't afford not to," Ms. Carver said. "That shark has brought us more publicity and more visitors in the past day than we usually have in a month! You saw the headlines and the crowds clamoring to get in here today. At last we have something to compete with the big fancy theme parks."

Mac's face was bright red with anger. "This isn't a theme park. It's a place where people care for and learn about ocean creatures."

"Without money, we can't care for any animals," Ms. Carver said.

"But that doesn't mean — " Mac began.

Ms. Carver waved her hand. "Don't worry. I have a plan to get some money for the park."

"What is it?" asked Mac.

Ms. Carver bit her lip. "I can't say. It's risky. But I think it's the answer to our problems." She looked at the tank. "And the shark's." With that, she turned on her heel and left.

Mac sighed heavily. He looked upset.

Emily and the children walked to where he was standing. "I guess she didn't agree with you," Emily said.

"No," Mac said, his voice weary. "She just doesn't get it."

"She doesn't know anything about animals. All she knows is money," Emily muttered angrily. "She's been cutting the budget anyplace she can. She cuts care for the animals, cuts people's salaries — she doesn't care who she hurts — " Emily stopped abruptly, as if realizing she'd said too much.

Mac looked at Mr. Alden and the children before replying. "That isn't quite fair. Ms. Carver only took over here a month ago, when her uncle left her the park in his will. She can't help it that she went to business school instead of studying animals. She's doing the best she can. But with attendance at the park dropping, we soon won't have the money to care for the animals properly." He ran his hand through his short hair. "If only I could figure out a way to do something." Mac walked off by himself, deep in thought.

The Aldens spent several more minutes watching the shark. Benny was fascinated — the shark was frightening, but in a strange way it was also beautiful.

"It's getting late," Emily said. "I'd better take you guys back to your cabin. Then I'll give you a lift to my dad's," she told Mr. Alden.

As they walked back to the cabin, Emily was quiet, thinking. Once inside the cabin, she turned to the Aldens and said, "I really shouldn't have said all those things about Ms. Carver. I don't want you to get the wrong idea. She and I have just had a bit of a rocky start since she came here."

"What do you mean?" Violet asked gently.

"I've worked here for five years, since when Ms. Carver's uncle was the director," Emily began. "He was a man who loved animals . . . but he didn't have the best business sense. That's why the park got into such bad shape in the first place. Ms. Carver is just the opposite. When she first came, she cut salaries because the park wasn't making enough money. Then she told me I didn't focus enough on my work — that I don't always have my mind on the animals. But that's not true! Ever since then I've been trying to prove her wrong."

"Sounds like a difficult situation," said Mr. Alden.

Emily looked at her watch. "I'd better take you to my dad's before it gets too late, Mr. Alden."

Grandfather gave each of the children a hug. "If you need me, Emily has the phone number," he said. "See you in a few days."

"I'll come by tomorrow morning," Emily told the children.

"Good night!" they called as Emily and Mr. Alden left.

The next morning, Emily arrived at the Aldens' cabin with a bag of bagels in her hands. "I've brought breakfast."

"Thanks," said Jessie. "But you don't need to provide all our meals. Grandfather gave us money for that."

"There's a grocery store right downtown," Emily said. "It's an easy walk. Have a bagel, and then I'll tell you how to get there. When you get back, you can join me at the Dolphin Arena."

A short while later, the Aldens were on their way into town. They'd passed the post office and a toy store when suddenly they spotted a group of people and a police car up the road. "What's going on up ahead?" Violet wondered.

When the Aldens got closer, they saw the police car was parked in front of a small store called Wilson's Jewelers.

"What's happening?" Jessie asked a woman who was standing nearby.

"It's just awful!" said the woman. "There was a burglary here last night!"

CHAPTER 3

The Key to the Mystery

"Excuse me, did you say a *burglary*?" asked Jessie.

"Yes, someone stole some diamond jewelry," the woman said. "The owner of the store, Pete Wilson, is talking to the police."

"Let's get a closer look," Benny said.

"I think we should stay out of the way," Jessie began, but Benny had already run right up to a pair of police officers who were speaking with Mr. Wilson. One of the officers was holding a small notebook and making notes in it.

"So you said there were several people in the shop last night?" the officer with the notebook asked.

"Yes, it was quite busy," said Mr. Wilson. "And my sales assistant was out sick, so I was on my own. Anyway, I locked up at the usual time and went home. When I came in this morning, I noticed one of the cases was unlocked. And a whole tray of diamond jewelry was missing."

"Looks like an inside job," one of the officers said. The other nodded.

Benny waited for the men to finish talking and then said, "Hello, I'm Benny Alden. Those are my two sisters and my brother. Maybe we can help. We're good at solving mysteries."

The officers smiled at Benny. "Thanks for offering, but I think we can handle it."

"Well, if you need us," Benny said, "we're staying at the Ocean Adventure Park."

Jessie caught up with her little brother. "Sorry for the interruption, officers," she said, taking Benny's arm. "We're going now."

As they walked off, Benny turned to his sisters and brother. "Can you believe it? A mystery!" The Aldens loved to solve mysteries.

"I think we'll let the police handle this one," Henry said, ruffling his brother's hair.

Benny looked disappointed. "Okay," he said softly. Then his face grew thoughtful.

"What is it?" Jessie asked.

"I was just wondering," Benny said. "I heard the police saying something about this looking like an 'inside job.' What does that mean?"

"That means that it was done by someone who works there," Jessie explained.

"I wonder why they think that," said Benny.

"Probably because there's no sign of someone breaking into the store," Henry said.

"That's true. I don't see any broken windows or anything," Benny said.

Violet had been walking off to one side. Suddenly, she stopped and bent to pick up something off the ground. She stood looking at the object for a moment, turning it over in her hands.

"What's that?" asked Jessie.

"It's a card key," said Violet. "One side is blank, but the other side says 'Ocean Adventure Park.' "

"That's like the key Emily used back at the park to get through the gate to our cabin," Jessie said.

"I think we'd better show it to the police," said Henry. "It may be evidence."

The Aldens started walking back toward the police officers, who were getting into their patrol car. Mr. Wilson had gone inside the store.

"Excuse me!" Jessie called, waving to the officers. "Excuse me!"

The officers had just shut their doors, and the Aldens heard the engine starting.

"Officer!" Henry cried out.

But they were too late. The police drove away.

"Oh, well," Henry said. "You know this key may not have anything to do with the burglary anyway."

WILSON'S JEWELERS

"You're right," Violet agreed. "Maybe whoever dropped it was here yesterday before the store was robbed."

"Maybe . . ." said Jessie. "But it does make me wonder."

"When we get back to the park, we'll take the key to the main office," Henry suggested. "Then whoever lost it can come claim it."

"Good plan," said Jessie. "Now let's go get our groceries."

The grocery store was two blocks farther down the main street. The children loaded up with eggs, milk, juice, bread, jam, butter, ham, cheese, and fruit. They also bought some spaghetti and a jar of sauce for dinner. Then, carrying their bags, they headed back to their cabin.

On the way, the Aldens stopped to drop off the card key at the main office. It was a small room with a counter containing brochures about the park. Behind the counter was a door leading into a smaller office. The sign on the door read, PARK DIRECTOR.

Ms. Carver came out of her office when she saw the Aldens come in.

"Yes?" she asked.

"Hello," Henry replied. "We found this card key someone must have lost." He placed it on the counter.

"Thank you," said Ms. Carver. "Where was it?"

"It was in front of Wilson's Jewelers," Jessie said.

Ms. Carver looked up sharply. "In front of Wilson's?" she repeated.

"Do you know that store?" Jessie asked.

"Yes," Ms. Carver said. "Mr. Wilson is . . . a friend of mine." She picked up the key and turned it over in her hands.

"The store was robbed!" Benny said.

"Really?" Ms. Carver said. "How terrible."

"Has anyone reported their key missing?" Henry asked.

"No, not yet," Ms. Carver said. "Actually, only a few people in the park carry this kind of card key — people at the director level. The others have blue card keys." She handed the key back to Henry. "You keep it. You'll need it to get in and out of your cabin and around the park."

"But what about the person who lost it?" Jessie asked.

"That's not your concern," Ms. Carver said. "But I do have extra keys for people who've lost them." Then she walked quickly into her office and closed the door.

Outside of the building, Violet said, "It was nice of her to give us the key."

"I don't know if *nice* is a word I'd use to describe her," Jessie said.

"No, she isn't very friendly," said Henry.

"We'll have to check back later and see if anyone came in to get a new key because they'd lost theirs," Jessie suggested.

"Do you think the person who lost the key is the one who robbed the store?" Benny asked.

"That might be," Jessie replied.

"Ms. Carver mentioned that only a few people have that kind of key," Henry pointed out. "Like Emily and Mac."

"I can't believe either of them would rob

the jeweler's," said Violet. "They could have just shopped there and dropped their card, you know."

"That's possible," said Jessie. "We can ask them."

The Aldens used their new key to open the gate leading to their cabin. After they'd put away their groceries, they went to the Dolphin Arena, where Emily had said she'd be. The arena was a small stadium with a pool of water in the center and rows of seats in a semicircle, sloping up from the pool.

The children followed the crowd of people who were entering the stadium.

"I wonder where Emily wanted to meet," Henry said, looking around.

The Aldens scanned the stands, looking for Emily. They didn't see her anywhere.

Just then, over the loudspeaker, they heard a familiar voice say, "And now, ladies and gentlemen, take your seats. The show is about to begin!"

The Aldens looked at the platform beside the tank and saw Emily in a bright blue bathing suit, holding a microphone and waving to the crowd.

"Cool!" said Benny. "She's doing the show!"

The Aldens quickly found seats a few rows up from the pool.

"Welcome to Ocean Adventure Park," Emily said. "I'm Emily Ballard, head animal trainer here at the park. I'd like to introduce two of my friends, Pearl and Rainbow."

She blew on a whistle that was hanging on a cord around her neck, and two sleek dolphins raced from the dolphin tank into the pool. They swam right up to the shallow end where Emily was standing. When Emily leaned over and made kissing noises, the dolphins lifted their heads to hers and gave her "kisses" on the cheek. The crowd cheered.

Emily reached into her hip pouch and pulled out some small fish, which she tossed to the dolphins. Then she swung her arm in a large arc and the dolphins raced around the pool, chasing each other. Suddenly, perfectly timed together, both dolphins leaped out with a giant splash, flipped in the air, and dived back into the water. The crowd roared with excitement.

"Aren't they wonderful?" Jessie said.

While the dolphins played, Emily talked to the audience. "Everybody knows dolphins live in water. Does that mean they're fish?"

Several voices shouted out from the audience. "Yes!" cried some people. "No!" shouted others.

"No, they're mammals!" shouted Benny.

Emily heard Benny's answer and smiled. "That's right, they're mammals just like us. They give birth to live babies instead of laying eggs. And they breathe air, instead of using gills. See that hole on top of their heads? They use it to breathe. It's called a blowhole."

Emily waved her hand above her head and the dolphins jumped in the air and sprayed water out of their blowholes.

"That looked like a fountain!" said Violet.

"Did you know that dolphins are some of the smartest animals around?" Emily asked the crowd. "They have many ways of communicating." Emily motioned and the dolphins came over to where she was standing. On command they made a series of different noises — clicks, whistles, even something that sounded like a person laughing. "That was great, guys," she told the dolphins, rubbing their heads affectionately and tossing them some more fish from her pouch.

"Scientists are working to understand what all of these sounds mean," Emily told the audience. She made another signal, and the dolphins dived underwater and smacked the surface loudly with their tails. "This is another way dolphins talk to one another," Emily explained. "Perhaps to warn others of dangerous animals nearby, like sharks."

"That is so cool," said Henry.

"Dolphins are so smart, they've been known to rescue people who are shipwrecked and save people from sharks. Some have been trained to help children who are physically or mentally challenged," Emily said.

"I didn't know they could do all that," whispered Violet.

Emily went on, "And they're also able to learn a lot of commands and signals, so they can do some neat tricks." She whistled and then held her arm up straight in the air. The dolphins came up out of the water as if standing on their tails. When Emily waved her arm in a circle, they spun around as if dancing. Then she swung her arm a different way. The dolphins went down in the water and swam very fast. All of a sudden they leaped out and touched a ball that hung from a wire high above the water. With each new trick the audience cheered more loudly.

Violet looked around at the cheering crowd. Suddenly, she noticed someone she'd seen before. He was sitting at the other end of their row, watching the dolphins perform. It was the man in the blue baseball cap who had watched them through the gate the night before.

Who was he? And why did he keep showing up where they were?

CHAPTER 4

Playing with Dolphins

"Jessie, look!" Violet whispered to her sister.

"What is it?" Jessie asked.

"Look down there!" Violet motioned with her head. "The man in the blue baseball cap."

"What about him?" Jessie asked.

"Remember, we saw him yesterday, and he seemed to be trying to get our attention?" Violet said.

Jessie wrinkled her forehead. "Oh, yeah, when we first got here."

"He stayed by the gate after Emily took us down the path to our cabin," Violet said. "He stood watching us for a long time."

"He did?" Jessie said.

"Yes, and now he's sitting right near us," Violet pointed out. "Does that seem a little . . . strange to you?"

"It could be a coincidence," Jessie said. But she knew what her sister was thinking — that the man was there for a reason. "Let's tell Emily about it after the show," she said.

The dolphins did several more tricks, but Violet wasn't able to concentrate. She kept wondering about the man in the hat.

The show ended with the dolphins waving good-bye with their flippers and blowing kisses at the crowd. As the dolphins swam away, the audience cheered with delight.

"Wasn't that great?" Benny said.

"It was," Jessie agreed. "It's amazing what the dolphins can do and how well they understand Emily."

Violet nodded her head absently. She

looked to see if the man in the baseball cap was still there. His seat was empty. She looked around but didn't see him anywhere. *Maybe he was just here to see the show*, she thought. *I'm probably just imagining there's more to it.*

Violet followed her brothers and sister down to the platform where Emily was standing.

"That was great!" Benny cried.

"I wish I could play with the dolphins like you did," Jessie said.

"Then go get your swimsuits on," Emily said.

The Aldens looked at Emily, their eyes wide. "Really?"

"Sure! I could use some helpers," Emily told them.

"We'll be right back!" Henry cried, as the children took off for their cabin to change.

Ten minutes later the Aldens were back, dressed in their swimsuits. Emily was standing at the far end of the arena.

"That was fast," Emily said. "Before I bring out the dolphins, there's something

I'd like you to try." She took off the whistle that was around her neck. "Which one of you would like to be the trainer first?"

"I will," said Jessie, stepping forward.

"All right," said Emily, handing her the whistle. "And who'd like to be the dolphin?"

The Aldens laughed.

"I will," Benny offered.

Emily smiled. "This will give you an idea of what it's like from the dolphin's point of view." She turned to Jessie. "I want you to teach Benny a trick, but you can't use words because dolphins don't speak our language. Instead you have to use hand signals and the whistle. And when he gets something right, you're going to reward him."

"Reward?" Benny asked.

"Yes," said Emily, turning to Benny. "What do you like?"

"Food!" said Henry, and everyone nodded.

"How about candy?" Emily suggested, pulling a small bag of chocolate candies from behind the platform. Benny nodded eagerly. "Okay, Jessie will give you one every time you get something right."

"This is kind of like training our dog, Watch," Jessie said. "We give him dog biscuits."

"You're right," said Emily. "Now let's see if you can train Benny."

Jessie blew the whistle, and Benny pretended to swim over. Jessie waved her hand in the air, and Benny tried several tricks he'd seen the dolphins do during the show. He jumped up in the air, spun around, and waved his arms like flippers. But Jessie just shook her head and repeated the arm motion again and again. Henry and Violet wondered what kind of trick Jessie was trying to teach Benny. But Jessie couldn't just *tell* Benny to do something.

"This is hard," Jessie said.

"You're telling me," said Benny, out of breath.

Emily grinned. "Now you know how hard the dolphins work, learning to understand us."

Benny laughed, and suddenly Jessie nodded and smiled. She pulled out a chocolate and handed it to Benny.

Benny's eyes lit up. He took the candy and ate it. Then he laughed again, and Jessie nodded and handed him another chocolate.

"You got it," said Emily. "Jessie wanted to make you *laugh*. That was the trick."

The children took turns playing the role of dolphin and trainer until they'd each had a chance. Then Emily said, "All right, I think you're ready. Follow me."

Emily took the Aldens over to the far end of the arena. She helped each of them put on a life jacket.

"One more thing," Emily added, handing them each a pouch of raw fish to hang around their necks. "You'll need these to reward them."

Benny made a face. "I liked my reward better."

"Now wait here," Emily said, leading them into the shallow end of the tank.

"Where are you going?" Benny wanted to know.

"To get some dolphins," Emily said, flashing a smile. She ran back to where the dolphin tank fed into the arena and opened the gate. A few minutes later, she was swimming back over to the Aldens with two sleek gray dolphins.

The children were so excited they could hardly speak.

"Henry, you and Violet can work with Pearl, and Jessie and Benny will work with Rainbow," Emily said. "Feel how soft they are."

The children stroked the dolphins' backs the way Emily had. "I've never felt anything so soft and smooth," said Violet.

Emily showed the children how to do the different hand motions they'd seen her do during the show. They raised their arms high, and the dolphins went up on their tails. They swung their arms, and the dolphins did flips. They made kissing noises, and the dolphins echoed them. For each trick, they rewarded the dolphins with fish and plenty of stroking.

Too soon, it was time for Emily to get ready for her next show. As the Aldens got out of the water, their faces glowed with happiness. Taking off their life jackets, they

all talked at once. "That was so great!" Henry said.

"I'm glad you enjoyed it," Emily said, her face glowing almost as much as the Aldens'. "Now you can see why I love my job so much."

"Thank you for letting us play with the dolphins," said Violet.

"No problem," Emily said.

As the Aldens toweled off, Jessie suddenly remembered something. "Emily?" she said. "Have you ever been to Wilson's?"

A look of recognition flickered across Emily's face for a moment, but then it was gone.

"Wilson's?" she repeated.

"It's a jewelry store in town," Jessie explained.

Emily looked at her watch and said, "I've got to run and grab something to eat before my next show. See you!" And with that she was off.

Jessie and Violet looked at each other. "That seemed sudden," Violet said.

"Yes, it did," Jessie agreed.

"And there was something about the look on her face," said Violet. "As if she was avoiding the truth."

"All I asked was if she'd ever been to Wilson's," said Jessie. "Why wouldn't she answer?"

"We didn't even get to ask her about the key," said Henry. "Let's stop by the office on the way back to our cabin and see if anyone's claimed it."

The office was empty when the Aldens entered. Ms. Carver's door was open a bit, and the children could hear her talking with someone inside, although they couldn't see who it was.

"Maybe if we wait a few minutes she'll be done," Violet suggested. As they stood at the counter, they couldn't help but overhear what Ms. Carver was saying.

Suddenly, she said something that made the children look at one another in horror.

"The only answer," Ms. Carver said, "is to kill the great white shark."

CHAPTER 5

Kill the Shark!

The Aldens couldn't believe what they had just heard. Had Ms. Carver really said she wanted to kill the shark?

The other person in the room with her murmured a response, speaking too softly for the children to hear.

"I know, I know," Ms. Carver went on. "I'm not happy about it, either. But it's simply too expensive."

Then, suddenly, Ms. Carver's door opened. The Aldens looked at one another, unsure what to do. Before they could say or do anything, Ms. Carver stepped out.

When she saw the Aldens, she looked surprised. And angry.

Then the person she was speaking with appeared in the doorway. The Aldens were surprised to see someone they recognized. It was Mr. Wilson. The children recognized him from that morning, when he'd been talking to the police outside his store.

"How long have you been standing here?" Ms. Carver asked.

"Just a couple minutes," Henry said.

"Were you listening to our conversation?" she demanded.

"No!" Jessie said.

"I certainly hope not," Ms. Carver said fiercely. She gave Mr. Wilson a look before turning back to the children. "What are you doing here, anyway?"

Jessie spoke up in a nervous voice. "We just, um, we just came to see if anyone had claimed the card key."

"No," said Ms. Carver. "No one has. Which is strange, because I can't imagine how someone could do their job without their key."

"That is odd," Jessie agreed, eager to escape. "Well, see you later!"

The Aldens hurried out of the office. When they were down the path a bit, Jessie turned to the others. "Can you believe what she said?"

"How could she kill the shark?" Violet asked in horror.

"And why was she talking about it with Mr. Wilson?" Henry added.

"We need to tell Emily right away," Jessie said. "I hope she's back in the arena."

The Aldens ran back to the Dolphin Arena, their sandals pounding the pavement. Emily was refilling her fish pouch when they ran in, breathless. She looked concerned when she saw their serious faces. "What is it?" she asked.

"We just overheard Ms. Carver saying something awful!" Jessie said.

"What?" Emily asked.

"She said she was going to kill the shark!" Henry said.

"She said *what*?" asked Emily.

"She said it was too expensive, and she'd have to kill it," Jessie said.

"She was in her office," Henry explained. "And when she came out, she asked if we'd heard what she was saying. We said no, because we didn't want her to get mad."

Emily thought for a minute. "I have a show coming up in a few minutes, but you guys need to tell Mac. He'll know what to do."

The Aldens ran to Mac's office, which was next to the great white shark's tank. They found Mac standing beside the tank, talking to some of the visitors who were crowded around watching the shark swim. Benny watched, too. The shark didn't scare him as much as it had the day before.

The Aldens waited, trying to be patient. At last Mac finished talking and came right over. "Is something wrong?" he asked.

The Aldens repeated what they'd told Emily. Mac shook his head. "Who was she speaking to?" he asked.

"It was Mr. Wilson, from the jewelry store downtown," Jessie said.

Mac frowned sharply.

"Do you know him?" she asked.

"Yes," said Mac. Then he added quickly, "I mean, I know the store."

"You've been there?" Henry asked, remembering the card key.

"A while ago," Mac said vaguely. Then he steered the conversation back to the shark. "I need to know exactly what you heard Ms. Carver say."

"She said, 'The only answer is to kill the great white shark,' " Henry repeated.

"You must have misunderstood," Mac insisted.

"Those were her exact words," said Henry. "She said she wasn't happy about it, but it was too expensive."

"That's terrible," said Mac. "I never thought that would happen here. . . ." His voice trailed off. "I'll go speak to Ms. Carver right away."

When Mac had left, the Aldens hung around the great white shark's tank, watching the huge animal glide slowly by. Its sheer size took their breath away each time it passed. The shark's glassy eyes stared off in an eerie way, never seeming to focus on the children the way other animals did, like the friendly dolphins. But the shark was alive — and someone wanted it dead.

The Aldens wandered over to the other shark tank and looked at the collection of smaller sharks swimming around the algae-covered rocks piled on the sandy bottom. The sharks were a range of sizes, colors, and shapes. Some had flat whiskered snouts and hovered close to the bottom of the tank. Others had more pointed mouths and swam near the top.

A few minutes later, Mac returned. "Ms. Carver wasn't in her office, but I left her a note," he said. "I'm sure there's an explanation."

Mac stood with the Aldens for a moment, watching the sharks.

"Sharks are cool," Henry said.

"Yes, they are," Mac agreed. "They've

been around for millions of years — since before the dinosaurs."

"Are these all sharks in this tank?" Violet asked.

"Yes," said Mac.

"But they look so different from one another," said Violet.

"There are hundreds of kinds of sharks, and they are very different," Mac said. "The ones in this tank aren't dangerous to people. See that bottom-feeder down there?" Mac asked, pointing.

The Aldens looked down toward one of the only piles of rocks that wasn't covered with algae. A shark hovered next to it. "That's a nurse shark. It's named that because it sucks on sand the way a baby sucks on a bottle, searching for clams or crabs to eat. When I first started working with sharks, I lost my balance and accidentally sat down on one of those."

"You did?" said Benny. "What happened?"

"Nothing," said Mac. "I was afraid it might be mad, but it just moved away. Despite what people think, sharks aren't out to get you." Mac pointed to one of the sharks higher up. "That's a sand tiger shark, and the one with the white patch on its fin is a white-tip reef shark." Mac checked his watch. "It's their feeding time now, if you'd like to help me."

"Sure," said Henry.

"Um . . . okay," said Benny quietly.

Mac gave each of the children a bucket of fish. They followed him up to a raised platform next to the tank and he showed them how to drop the fish in.

The Aldens watched the sharks grab the fish as they fell through the water, tearing at them with their sharp teeth.

"They still look pretty fierce," said Benny as he climbed down from the feeding platform.

"Sharks have a bad reputation as bloodthirsty killers," Mac said, "but actually, most species aren't dangerous to people at all."

"Hear that, Benny?" Jessie said. "He's been afraid of sharks ever since he saw the movie *Danger in the Deep*."

"That shark is dangerous, though," Benny said, running toward the larger tank, where the great white was swimming by itself.

"It's very rare for sharks to attack people," Mac said. "Each year only about fifty people *in the whole world* report being attacked by a shark. Sharks don't hunt people — it's just that sometimes they mistake a person for a seal, which is what they usually eat."

"In your book you said you'd been in the water with a great white shark," said Henry. "What's it like?"

A faraway look came over Mac's face. "It's an amazing experience," he said. "They're such beautiful, powerful animals. Once one bit me — but when it realized I wasn't its usual dinner, it swam away. I went right back in the water as soon as the wound healed."

"Weren't you scared?" asked Benny.

"I make sure to be careful," Mac said. "But I wouldn't let fear keep me from my exciting work. I did all kinds of research out in the open sea, swimming with all kinds of sea creatures."

"Do you go in the tanks with them here?" Jessie asked.

"We sure do," Mac said. "Not just me, but the other divers also. We have to clean the windows, do repairs, help injured animals, things like that. When we first brought the great white in, we had to walk it around the tank."

"You were in there with that shark?" Benny asked him, amazed. "Weren't you scared?"

"It's frightening, yes," Mac said. "But we had to keep the shark alive. Unlike other kinds of fish, sharks need to move, to have water go down their throats, in order to breathe. The shark was sluggish, so we took turns swimming it around, until it was swimming on its own."

Mac was silent for a moment. When he spoke again, his voice sounded weary and sad. "We worked so hard to keep this shark alive, and now someone wants to kill it."

As the others watched the great white shark, Violet went back to take another look at the other shark tank. She'd noticed something — something that was different from the way that tank had looked the day before. But she couldn't figure out what it was.

On their way back to their cabin, the Aldens stopped by the Dolphin Arena. Emily was in her small office next to the stands, looking through some papers on her desk.

"What did Mac say?" Emily asked as soon as she spotted the children.

"He went to speak to Ms. Carver but she was out," Henry said.

"She'd better have a pretty good explanation," Emily said.

"Are you all done here?" Jessie asked.

"Just about," Emily said. "That was my last show for the day. If you'll wait a minute, I'll walk back to the cabin with you. We can go as soon as I find my card key. It's been missing all day."

"It has?" Jessie said.

"Yes," Emily said, looking puzzled. "It's very strange. I never lose things."

"We found one in town," Violet said. "We didn't know who it belonged to, so we turned it in to Ms. Carver."

"Really?" Emily said quickly. "Where did you find it?"

"In front of Wilson's," said Jessie.

"Wilson's?" Emily repeated. A strange look flickered across her face.

"Have you been there lately?" Violet asked.

"Have I?" Emily said. "No, um — "

"It was robbed!" Benny interrupted.

"Oh, my goodness," Emily said. "Do the police know who did it?"

"No," said Benny, "but they said it looked like an outside job."

The other children laughed. "An *in*side job," Jessie corrected him.

"Oh, yeah," Benny said, his face turning red.

"What was stolen?" Emily asked.

"Some diamond jewelry," said Jessie.

"*Diamond?*" Emily asked.

"Yes," said Jessie. "Is something wrong?"

"No," Emily said. "It's just . . . I'm just surprised, that's all."

"So anyway, we found a card key there," Jessie said, pulling the key out of her pocket and showing it to Emily. "Ms. Carver said we could use it."

Emily took the key and turned it over. "No, this isn't mine."

"How can you tell?" Henry asked. "Don't they all look the same?"

"I put my initials on the back," Emily said.

"Why don't you just go get another card from Ms. Carver?" Violet suggested.

"Oh, well . . ." Emily paused. "I'm so busy. . . ."

"We could go ask her for you," Jessie offered.

"No!" Emily said quickly. Then she smiled. "I mean, that's okay. I'm sure mine will turn up. So — what are you guys doing for dinner tonight? I can give you the name of a great pizza place in town. I'd join you, but I've got some, um . . . things to do."

Jessie wondered why Emily was suddenly so eager to change the subject. But as usual, Benny was hungry. "Pizza sounds great!"

Emily grabbed a scrap of paper off her desk. "It's called Chariot Pizza. I'll write down the address for you," she said. "It's right off Stewart Avenue." Emily wrote something on the paper and then handed it to Jessie.

"Thanks," Jessie said, tucking the paper in her pocket.

Emily and the Aldens walked back to their cabins. "Tomorrow morning I can take you guys over to see the manatees, if you'd like," Emily suggested.

"Sounds fun," said Violet.

"What are manatees?" Benny asked.

Emily smiled. "They're a kind of sea animal. You'll see tomorrow."

When they reached the gate, Jessie used their card key to open it. As Emily headed into her cabin, she said, "Have a good dinner. Oh, and, um, don't mention to anyone that I lost my key, okay?"

"Sure," Jessie said. But she wondered why it was a secret.

A few minutes later, the Aldens had left the park and were headed toward town. "What street are we looking for?" Henry asked.

"I'll check," Jessie said, pulling the paper from her pocket and glancing at it. "Oh, that was nice — Emily gave us directions."

"I thought she just wrote down the address," Violet said.

"Me, too, but I guess she changed her mind," Jessie said. "Look how small and neat her handwriting is. It says, 'Turn right on Buffalo Street.' "

"Are you sure we don't turn left?" Henry asked. "Emily said Chariot Pizza was off Stewart Avenue, and that's the other direction."

"Her note says to go right," Jessie said.

"Okay," said Henry, as they turned the corner onto Buffalo Street.

"Why do you think Emily was so interested in the burglary at Wilson's?" Violet asked.

"Maybe she's just curious, like we are," Benny said.

"It seemed liked more than just curiosity to me," Jessie said.

"And I wonder why she doesn't want anyone to know she lost her card key," Henry put in.

"Maybe she wasn't telling us the truth," Jessie said. "Maybe this card *is* hers, but she doesn't want anyone to know she was near Wilson's."

"I can't believe Emily could be involved in the burglary," said Violet.

They had reached the corner of Buffalo and Main.

"Now it says, 'Turn right on Main Street,' " said Jessie.

"Hey, this is the way we came to the grocery store," Benny pointed out as they passed the post office and the toy store.

"You're right," Jessie agreed. "The directions say, 'Walk one block, and there you are.' "

The Aldens walked one block and stopped. They looked around, puzzled. There was no Chariot Pizza. There was no pizza restaurant at all. On one side of the street was an empty lot. On the other side was Wilson's Jewelers.

"This isn't where we're supposed to end up," said Henry.

"No, it's not," said Jessie. She looked at the note again and frowned. "This makes no sense at all. Listen to what it says next: 'Here's where we'll put our secret plan into action. See you there, Emily.' And then it's signed with the letter J."

"What?" asked Henry.

"Emily didn't write this," Jessie said, baffled. "This is a note *to* her from someone whose name starts with J."

"There's something on the other side of the note," said Benny.

Jessie turned the note over. "You're right," she said. "The back of the note says, 'Chariot Pizzeria, 110 State Street.' That's what Emily wrote. Her handwriting is totally different."

"Then what are those directions on the other side?" asked Violet.

"Someone must have written that note to Emily and it was lying on her desk," Henry said slowly, figuring it out as he talked. "She used the back of the paper to write the address we need."

"That makes sense," Jessie said.

"But then . . . what does it mean by a *secret plan*?" asked Benny.

"And," Violet added, "why do the directions lead straight to Wilson's Jewelers?"

CHAPTER 6

The Scene of the Crime

"This doesn't sound good," said Jessie.

"No, it doesn't," Henry agreed.

"I don't know about you guys, but I can't think straight on an empty stomach," Benny complained.

"All right, let's turn around and head back the way we came," said Henry. "I knew the pizza place was the other direction."

The Aldens retraced their steps. They found Stewart Avenue and spotted Chariot

Pizza right away. Fifteen minutes later they were sitting in a booth, munching on breadsticks while they waited for their pizza.

"Let's write down everything we know about this mystery," Jessie suggested, getting a small pad out of the backpack she always carried. "First of all, Wilson's was burglarized."

"Someone wrote a note to Emily saying something about a 'secret plan' and directing her to Wilson's," Henry said.

"Emily has lost her card key," added Benny. "And she doesn't want anyone to know."

"And we found a card key right outside Wilson's," said Jessie.

"Also, Emily seemed really interested in the burglary when we told her about it," said Henry. "Especially the diamonds."

The children stopped talking as a waiter brought over their pizza. For a few minutes everyone was silent as they each bit into a hot, cheesy slice.

"But why would she have robbed the jewelry store?" asked Violet after a moment.

PIZZA

"As they always say on TV detective shows, what's her motive?"

Everyone thought about that as they ate.

"Maybe it was for the money. She's said a couple of times that her salary is low, remember," Jessie said.

"I think we need to figure out who 'J' is," said Henry.

The door of the pizzeria opened, and the children were surprised to see who stood in the doorway. It was Emily, and she didn't look happy. She spotted the children immediately and walked over quickly.

"You found the restaurant," she said.

"Yes," said Jessie. "And the pizza's great, just like you said."

"Want to join us?" Violet asked, assuming that must be why Emily had come.

"No, I already ate," Emily said.

"Then, what . . . ?" Jessie began.

Emily looked around and then said, "Do you still have the piece of paper I gave you — with Chariot's address?"

"Yes," said Jessie, pulling it out of her pocket.

"I need it back," Emily said.

"Really? Why?" Benny wanted to know.

"It has something . . . important . . . on the back," Emily said. She shifted from foot to foot uncomfortably.

"We noticed there was something written there," Jessie said, handing her the scrap of paper.

"Yes, well, I need it back," Emily said. "Enjoy your pizza." She flashed a quick smile and was gone.

"Now, that was strange," Henry said. "Why did she need the paper back, unless it was something bad she didn't want us to see?"

"And why was she so nervous?" Violet added.

"I think we need to go back to the scene of the crime and see if we can find any more clues," said Jessie.

"Won't Wilson's be closed?" Violet asked.

"I noticed the sign on the door said it was open late tonight," Jessie said.

When they'd finished their pizza, the

Aldens walked back to Wilson's. As they walked, they talked about who else at Ocean Adventure Park might want to steal diamonds from the jewelry store.

"What about Ms. Carver?" Benny asked. "I don't like her at all. She isn't nice, and she wants to kill the shark."

"I don't like her much, either," said Jessie. "But that doesn't mean she's a thief."

"She is very concerned about money," Henry pointed out. "Emily said she's been cutting the budget to try to save money at the park. And it's obvious the park needs money — maybe stealing diamonds was how she planned to get it."

Suddenly, Violet spoke up. "Remember when she was talking to Mac? She said she had a plan to get some money! She wouldn't say what it was because it was risky. And that night Wilson's was robbed!"

"That's right," Jessie said. "And the card key we found could have been hers — that's why no one's come to claim it!"

"I hope she's the thief and not Emily," Benny said.

The children were just coming down the block toward Wilson's when suddenly Violet cried, "Look! Look who's coming out of the store!"

There were two men, deep in conversation. One was Mr. Wilson. With him was the man in the blue baseball cap.

"What's he doing here?" asked Jessie.

As the children approached the two men, they could hear bits of what they were saying. While they couldn't hear everything, they definitely heard the word "diamonds" several times.

Then the man in the baseball cap started to walk away. "Thanks, Pete," he said, waving to Mr. Wilson. "See you tomorrow."

Mr. Wilson waved and then walked back into the store. The man in the baseball cap got into a car that was parked by the curb and drove away.

"They seem pretty friendly," said Violet.

"They sure do," Jessie agreed. "Makes me think about what the police said, about this being an inside job. That means they think it was someone who either works here or was friendly with someone who does."

"Someone like that man?" asked Benny.

"Could be," said Jessie.

"Let's go inside," suggested Violet.

The Aldens entered the jewelry store.

Mr. Wilson was behind a counter when they came in. He smiled at the children. "How can I help you?"

"We're just, um . . . looking at bracelets," said Jessie, naming the first thing she saw in the display case.

"Silver?" Mr. Wilson asked.

Jessie nodded. Mr. Wilson came over and unlocked the back of the case. He pulled out a tray of silver bracelets. "Anything here you like?"

Just then the phone rang. "Excuse me a moment," Mr. Wilson said. "My assistant just left, so I'm all alone here." He went to get the phone, leaving the Aldens standing in front of the bracelet tray.

"Maybe that man was his assistant!" said Benny.

"Look over there." Henry pointed to a small alcove by the door. All of the display cases in the alcove held diamonds — rings, bracelets, earrings, necklaces. One shelf was completely bare. "That must be where the stolen jewelry was."

"It's right by the door," Jessie pointed out. "Easy to sneak out with."

Just then Mr. Wilson returned. "So what do you think?"

"Um, they're very pretty," Jessie said. "I need to think about it. I'll come back in a few days."

"All right," said Mr. Wilson, smiling and putting the tray back in the glass case.

As the Aldens were heading to the door, Henry stopped walking. He had his head down and looked as if he were thinking about something.

"What is it?" Jessie asked.

Without answering, Henry turned back to Mr. Wilson. "Um, excuse me, did we see you at Ocean Adventure Park today?"

"It's possible," Mr. Wilson said. "I was there today."

"I think we saw you in the office, speaking with Ms. Carver," Henry said, hoping

Mr. Wilson might explain what he and Ms. Carver had been discussing.

"I did have a meeting with her. We've been discussing some . . . plans," Mr. Wilson said. "How did you like the park?"

"It's great," Henry said. "Actually, we're staying there and helping out this week."

"How exciting," said Mr. Wilson. "I love that place. If I hadn't opened this shop, I would have loved to work with animals at a place like that. I visit there all the time."

"It is lots of fun," Jessie said.

"Well, thanks for your help," Henry said. "Good-bye."

As the Aldens walked back to town, Henry said, "I was hoping he'd tell us more about what he and Ms. Carver were discussing."

"Me, too," Jessie agreed. "He sounds like much too nice a man to want to kill a shark. He even said he wanted to work with animals."

The children walked in silence for a few moments. Then Henry said, "I was surprised he left that tray of jewelry out when he went to answer the phone."

"We wouldn't steal anything," Violet said.

"I guess he figured we were just children and we looked honest," said Henry. "Maybe that's what happened with the diamonds. Maybe he left some out, and something happened — like the phone rang — and he walked away. Remember, he told the police his assistant wasn't there that day, either."

"So someone stole the diamond jewelry while he wasn't looking?" Benny asked.

"Maybe," said Jessie.

"Sounds risky," said Violet. "That person must have had a good reason."

"*Risky*," Jessie repeated. "Just like Ms. Carver said."

CHAPTER 7

Save the Manatees!

The next morning, the Aldens went with Emily to the Manatee Haven.

"Have you spoken to Mac this morning?" Jessie asked. "Did he talk to Ms. Carver about the shark?"

"I haven't seen Mac yet," Emily said. "I'll stop by there later."

The Aldens decided not to mention the mix-up with the note from the night before, and Emily didn't bring it up, either.

"What's that baby bottle for?" Benny

asked when he saw what Emily was carrying.

"You'll see," Emily said, smiling mysteriously.

In the center of the large building was a giant tank. Swimming in the tank were two large animals and a slightly smaller one. They had fat, round bodies and looked a bit like walruses without tusks. They moved very slowly. Floating in the water were viny clumps of leaves, which they pulled into their mouths with their large front flippers.

"Are those manatees?" Benny asked.

"Yes, they are," said Emily.

"They're funny-looking!" he said.

"Not quite as sleek as the dolphins, are they?" Emily agreed.

"I think they're cute!" said Violet. "Like big roly-poly teddy bears."

"Manatees are gentle animals that graze on sea plants and grasses," Emily said. "Some people call them sea cows. The legends of mermaids may have started when sailors caught glimpses of manatees through the fog."

"Is that a baby one?" Jessie asked, pointing to the smallest of the three manatees.

"Yes," said Emily. "We brought him in because we found him alone, and he's too young to survive without his mother." Emily led the children to a platform beside the tank, from which she could reach the animals. "Come on, it's time for his breakfast."

The Aldens stepped up onto the platform and watched as Emily squatted by the edge and pulled the littlest manatee toward her.

Cradling the manatee's head, she fed it from the bottle.

"So that's what the bottle was for," said Benny.

"How sweet," said Violet.

Emily pointed to another one of the manatees. "See the scar on that one's back?"

"Is that from a shark attack?" Benny asked.

"No," Emily said. "Manatees are so large they don't really have any natural enemies, besides humans."

"People hunt manatees?" Violet asked.

"In some places people do, for meat and blubber oil," Emily said. "Manatees are endangered because people have destroyed the manatees' natural habitats. The scar on that manatee is from a speedboat. When people race around in speedboats where manatees live, the animals can get hurt."

"That's terrible!" Jessie said.

"Yes, it is," Emily agreed. "That's why some areas have passed laws protecting manatees and other wildlife."

"I wish there was something we could do," Jessie said.

When the manatee was done drinking from the bottle, it swam off in the water. Emily and the Aldens were watching the manatees when suddenly Emily said, "Oh, excuse me a minute." She darted up the path away from the Manatee Haven.

"Where did Emily go?" Benny asked.

"I don't know," said Henry. "Looked as if she saw someone she knew."

The Aldens looked where Emily had just gone and saw her deep in conversation with someone.

It was the man in the blue baseball cap.

"Him again!" said Violet.

"Does Emily know him?" Jessie asked, noticing that the man's hand was on Emily's arm.

"The other day she said she didn't," said Violet.

"Let's go see," said Jessie, starting up the path. But before the children could reach them, the man was walking away, and Emily was waving and calling out a friendly good-bye.

"It sure looks like she knows him," said Henry quietly.

A moment later, the Aldens came to where Emily was standing.

"Hello!" Emily said, smiling broadly.

"Hi," the Aldens replied.

"Who was your friend?" Jessie asked.

"My friend?" Emily said, her cheeks turning pink.

"That man we just saw — we keep seeing him around the park," Henry explained.

"Oh, he's . . . he's just a visitor here. He had a question," Emily said quickly. Then she changed the subject. "Did you guys like the manatees?"

"Yeah, they were really neat!" said Benny.

"How about checking out the penguins next," Emily suggested. "It's about time for them to be fed."

"Sure!" the children cried.

"Then let's go." Emily took off at a quick pace.

The Aldens looked at one another. They were excited to see the penguins, but they couldn't help feeling that Emily had changed the subject awfully quickly. Why? Was that man really just a normal visitor? It had looked as if he and Emily knew each other quite well. If she was telling the truth, then why was Emily's face so pink? And why had she said earlier that she didn't know him?

As the Aldens headed off after Emily, Henry whispered, "We've got to find out who that man is. I can't help feeling he has something to do with the burglary."

"Could he be the one who wrote Emily that note?" Benny asked. "J?"

"I wonder," said Jessie, stopping in her tracks to think.

"How could we find out?" Violet asked, her voice quiet but urgent. "We asked Emily, and she said he was just a visitor."

"What do we know about J?" Jessie asked quickly.

"He wanted Emily to go to Wilson's for a secret plan," said Henry.

"And he has neat handwriting," said Violet.

"That's it!" Jessie said excitedly.

"What?" the others asked.

"I have an idea," Jessie said. "I'll tell you later."

The Aldens caught up with Emily in front of the Penguin House. She led them in through a door marked EMPLOYEES ONLY.

"Here," Emily said, taking bright blue jackets from a closet and handing them to the children.

"What are these for?" asked Benny. "It's hot outside."

"But it's cold in the penguins' tank,"

Emily said. "Remember, they're from Antarctica, so they like it cold."

A burst of cold air flew out when Emily opened the door to the penguin enclosure. The Aldens were glad they'd put the jackets on. In front of them, the penguins stood in groups along the banks of a pool of water. The wall opposite the door they'd entered was glass, allowing visitors to look in. The Aldens could see a crowd gathered on the far side of the glass. Benny waved to them, a big smile on his face.

Emily had brought in some buckets of fish. The penguins crowded around her, eager for food. She gave each of the Aldens some raw fish, which they tossed to the hungry penguins.

"How cute they are!" said Jessie.

"I love the way they waddle," Violet said.

Once the penguins had eaten, some dived into the water and swam around, paddling with their short wings.

"I'm getting cold," Violet said.

"Me, too," Emily agreed. "Let's get going."

"I think it's feeding time for humans now," Benny said, and they all laughed.

Emily walked the Aldens to the snack bar, then left to do her afternoon dolphin show. As they munched on their hot dogs and fries, Henry said, "Jessie, you said you had an idea about how to find out if the man in the baseball cap is J. What is it?"

"First I need a pad of paper," Jessie said. She began to dig in her backpack.

"What are you going to do?" Henry asked.

"You'll see," said Jessie. A moment later, she pulled out a large yellow pad and a pen. She turned to a blank page and began to write. The others crowded around her to see what she was writing.

At the top of the page Jessie printed, SAVE THE MANATEES! in large, bold letters.

Underneath she wrote neatly, "Our government needs to pass laws to limit the use of motorized boats, in order to protect the endangered manatees."

Beneath that she signed her name and wrote her address. Then she handed the pad to Henry.

"What's this?" he asked.

"It's a petition," Jessie said. "To save the manatees. We'll send it to the governor."

"That's very nice," Henry said, "but what does it have to do with J?"

"You'll see," Jessie said mysteriously. "Just sign it, please."

When they had all signed their names, Jessie tucked the pad into her backpack. She looked at her watch. "If we want the plan to work, we'd better get going."

"Where?" Violet asked.

"To the Dolphin Arena," Jessie said.

They arrived just as Emily's show was ending. Jessie led the others to a bench outside the entrance. "I hope he's here," she muttered to herself, watching the crowds file out of the arena. She stepped forward and showed her pad to several people, who eagerly signed the petition. "Where is he?" Jessie muttered under her breath.

"Who?" asked Benny.

"The man in the baseball cap," Jessie said.

"How do you know he'll be here?" asked Violet.

"Just a hunch," said Jessie. "I think he likes Emily's shows."

They did not have to wait long. Soon a familiar man in a blue baseball cap emerged from the arena.

Jessie approached him quickly, her pad and pen in her hand. "Excuse me, sir," she said politely, handing the pad to him. "Would you sign my petition and put your address?"

The man smiled at Jessie. "Let me take a look," he said. He quickly read what Jessie had written.

"Sure, I'll sign," he said agreeably, taking the pen and writing his name and address.

"Thanks," said Jessie.

As the man walked away, Jessie glanced at the pad and then went back to where the others were sitting. She had a big grin on her face.

"We've gotten lots of signatures to help the manatees," Jessie said, pleased her plan had worked. She held the pad out to the others. "Best of all, we've found J."

CHAPTER 8

The Secret Plan

The Aldens all looked at the petition Jessie had made. There, at the bottom of the page, was the name John Quinn, along with an address. It was written in the same neat handwriting that had been on Emily's note.

"So if he's the one who wrote the note," Henry said, "Emily does know him — and pretty well, it seems. So why was she pretending she didn't?"

"I'm worried about what the 'secret plan' at Wilson's was," said Jessie.

"They couldn't be the burglars," Violet cried. "I just can't believe that."

"I agree," said Jessie. "But then why do all the clues point to Emily?"

"What clues?" asked Emily, who had just then come up to the Aldens without their noticing.

"You didn't rob Wilson's, Emily, did you?" Benny burst out.

Emily looked surprised. "Rob the jewelry store? What are you talking about?"

The children looked at one another, their faces pink with embarrassment. No one knew what to say.

Finally, Jessie began, "Well, we found a card key near the store, and you lost yours, and you didn't want anyone to know."

"And then on the back of that piece of paper yesterday was a note leading us to Wilson's, and it mentioned a secret plan," Henry said.

"And then we figured out who J was, but you kept saying you didn't know him," Violet put in.

"But you didn't really do it, did you?" Benny asked.

Emily had been listening to the children quietly. Suddenly, she burst into laughter. "Oh, my goodness, you *are* detectives, just as your grandfather said. I guess I have been acting a little strange lately, but I can explain. Hold on a minute."

Emily walked away and came back a moment later with the man in the baseball cap. "I guess I should have introduced you guys sooner. This is John," she said. "And these are the Aldens."

The Aldens said hello.

"John is my . . . fiancé," Emily said, taking his hand. She and John smiled at each other.

"Your what?" asked Benny.

"John and I are going to get married," Emily explained. "But I haven't told anyone here yet."

"That's such wonderful news," Violet said. "Why not share it?"

"Remember, I told you Ms. Carver said

I wasn't focusing enough on my work?" Emily said. "Well, I didn't want her to think I have my mind on John instead. So when I'm at work, I try to pretend he's just a regular visitor, instead of my fiancé. I don't want to lose my job."

"But I just can't stay away," John said, putting an arm around Emily. "I love watching Emily work."

"What was that note all about?" Jessie asked.

"Oh, that," said Emily. "When John and I had decided to get engaged, he left that note for me to follow — like a treasure hunt."

"We love those," said Benny.

Emily glowed with pleasure as she told the children what had happened. "It was fun. I followed the directions and found myself at Wilson's, where we picked out the most beautiful diamond ring." She and John smiled at each other.

"So the engagement was your secret plan," said Jessie.

"Why did you want the note back?" Henry asked.

"I'm going to put it in my scrapbook to remember always," Emily explained. "When I realized I'd accidentally given it to you, I was so upset."

"Can we see the ring you picked?" asked Violet.

"It's still at the store, being sized to fit my finger," Emily said. "That's why I was worried when you told me that the diamond jewelry had been stolen."

"I stopped by yesterday," John told Emily reassuringly. "Mr. Wilson said your ring is safe."

"So that's why you were there," said Benny.

"Emily, maybe you lost your key when you were ring-shopping," Jessie suggested.

"No, the key you found wasn't mine," Emily said. "It didn't have my initials on it."

"Why not just get another key from Ms. Carver until yours turns up?" asked Henry.

"If Ms. Carver knew I'd lost my key,

she'd take that as proof I wasn't paying enough attention to my work," Emily said.

"Now that we've answered all your questions, how about explaining that petition?" John said.

"Oh, that," Jessie said. "We thought you might be the one who'd written the note to Emily. I figured I could help the manatees — and also see your name and handwriting." Jessie smiled, proud of her plan.

"Very clever," said John.

"But we still don't know whose key we found," said Henry.

"Or who robbed the jewelry store," Benny added.

"But at least we know you're not the burglar," Violet told Emily.

"No, I'm an animal trainer," she said, smiling broadly. "And I'd better get back to work." She gave John a quick kiss good-bye and headed back into the arena. John waved to the kids and walked off.

"At least part of the mystery is solved," said Violet.

"Let's go see if Mac has heard from Ms.

Carver," suggested Henry, leading the way to the shark area.

When they got there, they were surprised to find not only Mac, but also Ms. Carver.

"I have some exciting news," she said. "We're bringing a new attraction to the park — an orca."

"But that's impossible!" Mac said.

"What's an orca?" asked Benny.

"It's a killer whale," Mac said. "They're huge — bigger than the great white shark. We don't have a tank big enough — "

Ms. Carver just smiled more and more broadly the whole time Mac was talking. Finally she interrupted him. "Don't worry, I'm not talking about an animal. I'm talking about a roller coaster."

"A roller coaster?" Mac said.

"Yes," Ms. Carver said. "It will be black and white, to look like an orca. I can see the posters now: 'Try Orca — It's a Whale of a Ride!' "

"That sounds great," said Henry.

"We love roller coasters," Jessie agreed.

Mac looked as if he didn't like the idea. "But this park has always been about animals, not carnival rides."

"We've got to change with the times, Mac," Ms. Carver told him.

"How are you planning to pay for this new ride when we can't even fix up the animals' tanks?" Mac asked.

"That's the whole point," Ms. Carver said. "The Orca will bring in more visitors, and that will raise money to fix up the rest of the park."

"But first you'll need money to *build* the ride," Mac pointed out. "How are you going to raise that?"

"I have my ways," Ms. Carver said mysteriously. "*I'll* worry about the money and you just worry about the animals." And with that, she walked away.

"That's exactly what I am worried about," Mac said softly to himself. Mac turned to the kids. "It's feeding time—want to help?"

"Sure," said Henry.

Jessie ran to put her backpack in Mac's

office so it wouldn't get wet. Mac picked up several buckets of raw fish and handed one to each of the Aldens.

The children followed Mac to the shark tank. For a change, Benny led the way, eager to see the sharks. As they walked, Henry said to Jessie, "How do you think Ms. Carver is planning to raise the money?"

"That's just what I was wondering," Jessie said. "Do you think it has anything to do with stolen diamonds?"

The children stopped talking as they arrived at the shark tank. Like the day before, they tossed handfuls of fish into the water. Suddenly they heard a loud thump coming from the great white's tank.

"Oh, no," Mac said, putting down his bucket and running over there.

"What was that?" Henry asked as he and the other children followed Mac.

Mac was standing by the tank, watching the great white shark swim. He looked worried.

"What happened?" asked Jessie.

"I was afraid this was going to happen,"

Mac said. "Remember I told you great whites don't do well in aquariums? They are extremely sensitive to electrical charges. The metal parts of the tank give off an electrical charge, and that can affect a shark's swimming. Other great whites in captivity have had this problem, too — they start bumping into the walls."

"What's going to happen?" asked Violet.

"I don't know," Mac said. "I think the only answer is to return this shark to the ocean. But you heard how Ms. Carver feels about it." Mac sighed. "Come on, let's rinse and put away the buckets."

The Aldens walked with Mac to the supply shed, where he unlocked the door with his card key. When everything was put away, Henry asked if there was anything else they could do.

"No, thanks," Mac said. "I've got some thinking to do." He looked very depressed, and the children decided they should go.

"I just have to get my backpack out of your office and then we'll go," Jessie told Mac.

Mac walked with Jessie to his office while the others stood by the tank, watching the sharks.

Mac tossed his card key onto his desk. "I'll see you later," he said, walking quickly out of the office, as Jessie hoisted her backpack onto her back.

Poor Mac, Jessie thought. She glanced at the card key on the desk. *At least we know he isn't the one who lost his card key at Wilson's.*

But as she began to walk out, she realized something that made her stop. Something about Mac's card was different. She turned back to the desk and looked at it again.

Something was written on the corner of the card. Jessie picked up the card to look at it more closely. There, in the corner, were the letters EB, handwritten with a pen.

EB? Jessie thought. *What does that stand for?* They weren't Mac Brody's initials. That would be MB.

EB . . . Emily Ballard! Jessie realized suddenly. Emily had said she'd written her initials on her card key. This must be it. That explained why Emily hadn't been able to find hers — Mac had it.

But what was he doing with it?

Was he using Emily's because he'd lost his own at Wilson's?

Jessie quickly laid the key on Mac's desk. Should she ask Mac about it?

No, she didn't want him to think she'd been poking around on his desk looking at his personal things. And anyway, what would she say to him? *Did you take Emily's card?* She couldn't say that.

She'd have to tell her sister and brothers. Together they'd figure out what to do.

Jessie hurried out to where the others were standing, watching the sharks in the tank.

They seemed to be studying something.

"What are you looking at?" Jessie asked.

Violet turned around. "I just remembered that when we were here yesterday, I noticed something strange." She pointed

into the tank. "See how all the rocks have algae on them?"

"Yes," Jessie said.

"Now look at those rocks over there." Violet pointed to the other side of the tank.

The rocks where Violet was pointing were perfectly clean.

"That's strange," Jessie said.

"It is," Violet agreed. "As if those rocks were just recently added."

"But why would someone have just added them?" Jessie asked.

"I don't know," Violet said.

Benny and Henry had walked to the other side of the tank, to see if they could find anything else unusual. Suddenly Benny shouted, "There's something behind the rocks! Come look!"

Jessie and Violet ran over. They looked where their brother was pointing. Sharks swam by, still grabbing at the fish that had been tossed into the tank for their dinner. But then the area cleared, and she saw it. Squeezed behind the rocks was a dark blue bag.

"A bag," Henry said.

"That would explain why those new rocks were added," Jessie said. "To hide that bag."

"What's in the bag?" Violet asked. "Why would it need to be hidden?"

"I don't know," said Henry, "but I think we need to find out."

"It's a hidden treasure!" Benny shouted.

"Maybe it's just . . . I don't know, something for the fish," said Violet.

"Could be," said Jessie. "Or maybe it's a bag of diamond jewelry."

"Do you really think that?" Violet asked.

"Well, listen to this." Jessie told the others about the card key she'd found on Mac's desk.

"So you think Mac stole the jewelry and hid it in the tank?" asked Violet. "And he borrowed Emily's card key so no one would know he'd lost his at Wilson's?"

"Looks that way," said Jessie.

"But he's such a nice man," said Violet.

"It is hard to think of him as a thief,"

Henry agreed. "But it makes sense. It all depends on what's in the bag."

"How do we find out?" asked Benny. "Jump in the tank with all those sharks?"

"They just had their dinner, so they probably wouldn't eat you," Violet joked, putting her arm around Benny.

"Very funny," Benny grumbled.

"Let's go tell Emily," Henry said. "She'll know what to do."

The Aldens hurried to the Dolphin Arena, where Emily had just finished the last show of the day. She was pulling a T-shirt over her bathing suit when the Aldens arrived.

"Hey, guys," Emily called out.

"We need your help!" Jessie said.

"What's up?" Emily asked, sitting down on a bench and giving them her full attention. The Aldens told Emily about the card key and the bag hidden behind the rocks in the shark tank. When they finished talking, she sat silently, looking stunned. "Mac?" she said at last. "I can't believe it."

"Neither can we," said Jessie.

"Show me the bag," Emily said, standing up and heading toward the shark tank at a brisk pace.

A few moments later, they were in front of the shark tank. Mac was nowhere to be seen.

"See?" Henry said, pointing. "Behind that rock."

"I see it," said Emily, nodding.

"What do you think that is?" Jessie asked.

"I have no idea," Emily said. "There's one way to find out. I'll have to go in there and see."

"Have you ever been in the shark tank before?" Violet wanted to know.

"No," said Emily. She didn't look pleased at the thought. "Mac and his staff handle this tank. At least it's not in that tank." She jerked her head toward the great white shark's enclosure.

"Are you going in right now?" Benny asked.

"No," Emily said. "I can't just go in the

tank with all these visitors here. Also, I don't want to accuse Mac of something if he didn't do it. We'll have to wait until the park's closed, when no one's around."

The Aldens nodded silently, their eyes wide.

Emily smiled. "Go back to your cabin and have some dinner. I'll come by after dark to get you."

CHAPTER 9

Swimming with Sharks

Time seemed to move slowly that evening. The Aldens had cooked and eaten their spaghetti and were playing cards to keep busy when there was a knock at the door. It was Emily.

"Come on," she said.

It felt strange walking through the park after hours. Only a few lights were on, and all the pathways were empty. Shadows lurked everywhere — behind benches and bushes and in the corners of the animals' tanks. Everything was silent and eerie.

When an owl cried in the distance, the children jumped.

The shark enclosure was dark. Emily had brought a flashlight with her, and she turned it on as they entered the building. "I don't want to turn on the lights and alert everyone that we're here," she explained.

The shark tank was even scarier at night than during the day. Through the dim water, they could just make out the shapes of the sharks as they moved through the water.

Emily shone the flashlight into the tank, searching for the rocks without algae and the mysterious blue bag behind them. "That's it," she said. "Henry, you take this." She showed him where to hold the flashlight, so it was shining on the bag. "I'm going in. Wish me luck."

Emily climbed into the tank. The Aldens watched as she swam down to the rocks. Shadows of sharks moved past her in both directions.

"Look!" Benny gasped as one of the

larger sharks swam up behind Emily, close enough to touch her.

"Don't worry, Benny," said Jessie. "Remember what Mac told us?"

Benny frowned, trying to remember. "He said these sharks won't hurt people."

"That's right," Jessie said. "He and the divers go into the tank to clean the glass and make repairs, remember?"

"Yes," said Benny softly. His eyes remained fixed on Emily. He watched as she moved the clean rocks and pulled out the dark blue bag. She swam quickly to the surface. A moment later, Emily climbed out of the tank, the bag in her hand. "Got it!" she said.

"All right!" cried Henry.

Benny looked relieved. "You're brave," he told her.

Emily squatted down on the floor, holding the bag in front of her. The Aldens crowded around and Henry shone the flashlight's beam on the bag. Emily untied the top and looked inside.

"What's in there?" Jessie asked.

"I don't know," Emily said, reaching in and pulling out a lumpy cloth bundle. Emily slowly unrolled the cloth as everyone leaned forward to see what was inside.

"Oh, my goodness!" cried Emily. There in her hands were several large pieces of jewelry — pins, earrings, necklaces, and rings, all studded with large sparkly diamonds.

"It really is the jewelry!" said Jessie. It was hard to believe their suspicions had been correct.

"Each one of those probably costs thousands of dollars," said Henry.

"Do you think Mac took them?" asked Violet, her voice trembling. "Maybe it was someone else — one of the other divers?"

"No, it was me," came a voice through the darkness. Henry quickly shone the beam in that direction. There, in the doorway, stood Mac.

Suddenly, the lights were flicked on. Ms. Carver had entered beside Mac. "What in heaven's name is going on?" she asked.

"Mac and I were in my office when we saw lights in the shark enclosure. What are you doing here?"

"I can explain," said Emily.

"No, I'm the one who needs to explain," said Mac. His voice sounded weary, as if he were carrying a heavy burden. "I stole the jewelry from Wilson's and I hid it here in the shark tank."

"You did *what*?" Ms. Carver said, gasping.

"I know, it's crazy," Mac said, shaking his head slowly. "I can't believe I did it myself. I don't know what came over me." He sighed deeply before going on.

"It was Monday—you kids had just arrived." Mac looked at Ms. Carver. "I wanted to let the shark go, but you said the park needed it, needed the money. I thought that was crazy."

"And robbing a jewelry store isn't crazy?" asked Ms. Carver.

Mac shrugged. "I didn't really plan for it to happen. When I left here that day, I was very upset. My wife had asked me to stop at Wilson's on the way home to pick up a watch she'd had repaired. Mr. Wilson was helping me, when suddenly a noisy group of customers came in. He went to help them — he was the only one working in the store that night — and I noticed the door to the diamond case had been left open."

Mac frowned as he remembered. "It just seemed so easy. I'd take the diamonds, sell them somewhere, and donate the cash to the park." Mac shook his head again. "And it *was* easy. No one was looking and the diamonds are kept in a separate alcove. I had my gym bag with me, so I just pulled out a tray of jewelry and slipped it into my bag." He swallowed hard. "And that was that."

No one said anything for a moment. At last Mac went on. "I knew immediately that what I'd done was wrong. But it was too late. All I could think of was to hide the jewelry for now. I planned to return it later. I thought I had time to figure out how to return it without anyone knowing. But I didn't count on our visitors being such good detectives." He smiled weakly at the Aldens.

"So that was your card key we found outside of Wilson's," said Jessie.

"Yes," said Mac, turning to Ms. Carver. "I was afraid that if I came to you for a new one, someone would connect me to the crime scene."

"So you borrowed mine," said Emily.

"I'm sorry," Mac said. "I assumed you would just get a new one. Since you had no connection to the burglary, it wouldn't matter to you."

"But I didn't want to get a new card because . . ." Emily's voice trailed off. Then she continued. "Because I didn't want you to think I'd lost mine, Ms. Carver. I didn't want you to think I wasn't focused enough on my job."

"I made that accusation before I got to know you," Ms. Carver said, "when I first started here. I've since learned what an excellent job you do and just how seriously you take your work."

Emily blushed with pleasure.

Ms. Carver's attention turned back to Mac. She hadn't said a word while he'd been telling his story. She had just listened, her face pained. “I’m shocked at you, Mac. You broke the law.”

“I did,” Mac agreed, his head down.

Ms. Carver sighed. “Your desire to help the shark was good, but that doesn’t make it okay to steal.”

Mac nodded sadly.

“You didn’t have to steal money to help the animals,” Ms. Carver added. “That’s why I’m building the new Orca ride. I was going to build two rides. The second was going to be called the Shark. But I had to kill that idea when I realized there wasn’t enough money to build both.”

“So that’s what you meant!” Henry said. “We were afraid you were going to kill the great white shark!”

“Good heavens, no!” said Ms. Carver. “Why would I do that?”

“It’s happened in another aquarium,” Mac said. “And, well, you don’t seem to care much about the animals.”

“That’s where you’re wrong,” Ms. Carver said. “I care so much about them that I don't want this park to close. This park does a lot of good for animals by teaching people about them. That's why I'm building the roller coaster — people may come for the rides, but they'll end up learning about our ocean creatures."

"I didn't like the idea of a roller coaster at first," Mac admitted. "But if it will keep this park alive, then I'm all for it."

"Ms. Carver, why did you say the way to get the money was risky?" Jessie asked.

"I'm investing my own money and a friend's in the ride," Ms. Carver explained. "If the park does well, we'll get our money back. But if attendance at the park doesn't improve, we might lose our money. So he and I are taking a risk."

"Oh, I get it," Jessie said.

Now Ms. Carver turned to Mac. "And you'll be interested to know that the other investor is Pete Wilson."

"Really?" said Mac.

"Yes," Ms. Carver said. "He's always been interested in Ocean Adventure Park. That's why he wants to donate money for the ride.

And that's why I'm hoping he won't go to the police when we tell him why you stole the diamonds, Mac."

"I know what I did was wrong and I'll cooperate with the police if it comes to that," Mac said. "But there's something else we need to talk about. The great white shark needs to go back to the ocean. He's been banging into the sides of his tank. So far, he's been okay. But if he hits the wall too hard, he'll die. We've already kept him alive in the tank much longer than I'd expected."

"All right," Ms. Carver said. "Come back to my office and we'll talk about it."

CHAPTER 10

No More Fears

"Good morning!" called a friendly voice.

Benny woke up and rubbed his eyes. Mr. Alden was standing in the doorway.

"Grandfather!" shouted Benny, jumping out of bed and running to give Mr. Alden a hug. Henry sat up in bed and grinned sleepily at his grandfather. A moment later, Jessie and Violet had joined them, and everyone seemed to be talking at once.

"When did you get here?" Jessie wanted to know.

"We helped feed the sharks," Benny told him.

"We swam with the dolphins," Henry added.

"We missed you!" Violet was saying.

Grandfather smiled broadly. "It's good to see you all. Sounds like you've been having lots of fun."

At last the children quieted down. "We *have* been," Jessie said.

"What time is it?" Henry asked, noticing the bright sunlight streaming in the window.

"You slept late this morning," Grandfather said. "I took a taxi here from my friend's house. I was sure you'd be up by now."

"It was a late night last night," Henry said.

"We were solving a mystery!" cried Benny.

"Ah . . . I knew there had to be a mystery," Mr. Alden said, smiling. "I want to hear all about it. But first, how about some breakfast — although it's nearly lunchtime."

The Aldens put together a delicious breakfast in their little kitchen. There were scrambled eggs, toast with jam, sliced fruit, and juice to drink. The children took turns telling their grandfather what had happened during the few days they'd been apart.

At last the story of the burglary, Emily's engagement, the roller coaster, and the great white shark had all been told.

"I can't believe all that took place in such a short time!" said Grandfather.

"I wonder what will happen to the great white shark," said Henry.

"Let's find out!" Jessie said.

The children dressed quickly and headed over to the shark enclosure. When they got there, they were surprised and saddened to find the large tank held nothing but water.

Grandfather and the children stood silently, staring at the large empty tank. A few minutes later, Mac emerged from his office. He looked tired. But for the first time, his face looked calm. The Aldens realized now how worried he'd been during the past week.

"What happened to the shark?" Benny asked.

"We took him back to the ocean," Mac said.

"Already?" Jessie asked.

"I didn't know how much longer he'd make it in a tank," said Mac. "We took care of it during the night."

"Now he'll be okay?" Violet asked.

"Yes," Mac said firmly. "He'll be fine."

Emily and John walked up, holding hands. "Morning!" they called out.

"This must be John," Mr. Alden said.

"So you've heard about me," John said, grinning.

"What happened with the jewelry?" Henry asked Mac.

"I spoke with Mr. Wilson," Mac said. "Ms. Carver and I went there first thing this morning."

"What did he say?" Henry asked.

"He was glad to have the jewelry back," Mac said. "I'm going down to the police station now to turn myself in. I just wanted to tie up a few loose ends here."

"What's going to happen to you, Mac?" Benny asked, worried.

"I don't know," Mac replied. "I have to pay for what I did. But I hope that if I cooperate, the judge won't be too hard on me."

Jessie ran up and gave Mac a big hug. The others followed.

Grandfather and Mac shook hands. "Good luck," Mr. Alden said. Mac waved to the children and walked off.

"I was thinking that maybe today you kids might like to take a break from the park," Mr. Alden said to his grandchildren. "How does a day at the beach sound?"

"Great!" the children all shouted.

"We'll join you," Emily said.

"Don't you have to work?" Jessie asked.

"I don't have to focus on my work today," Emily said, grinning. "It's my day off."

Mr. Alden took his youngest grandchild aside and looked him in the eye. "What about you, Benny?" he asked quietly. "Still afraid?"

Benny thought for a moment. "I've learned a lot about sharks, Grandfather. I'm not afraid anymore."

GERTRUDE CHANDLER WARNER discovered when she was teaching that many readers who like an exciting story could find no books that were both easy and fun to read. She decided to try to meet this need, and her first book, *The Boxcar Children*, quickly proved she had succeeded.

Miss Warner drew on her own experiences to write the mystery. As a child she spent hours watching trains go by on the tracks opposite her family home. She often dreamed about what it would be like to set up housekeeping in a caboose or freight car — the situation the Alden children find themselves in.

When Miss Warner received requests for more adventures involving Henry, Jessie, Violet, and Benny Alden, she began additional stories. In each, she chose a special setting and introduced unusual or eccentric characters who liked the unpredictable.

While the mystery element is central to each of Miss Warner's books, she never thought of them as strictly juvenile mysteries. She liked to stress the Aldens' independence and resourcefulness and their solid New England devotion to using up and making do. The Aldens go about most of their adventures with as little adult supervision as possible — something else that delights young readers.

Miss Warner lived in Putnam, Connecticut, until her death in 1979. During her lifetime, she received hundreds of letters from girls and boys telling her how much they liked her books.